D1522020

HARREN PRESS PRESENTS

SHERLOCK HOLMES

AND THE CASE OF THE MAN-MADE VACUUM

Roy C. Booth and Nicholas Johnson

Sherlock Holmes
and the Case of the Man-Made Vacuum

Edited by Samantha Lafantasie
Cover Art/Design by Nick Bastin

Table of Contents

Dedications:

From Roy: To Eric M. Heideman, See you on the Holmesian panels, old boy!

From Nicholas: To Erica. For everything.

Acknowledgements

Roy thanks Nick, John, Roger, Geoffrey, Eric, Bob, Brian, the other Brian, William, Paul, Cynthia, Mitch, Mike, Abbey, Louise, and Axel – The Legion of Booth.

Nicholas would like to thank Roy and Cynthia, Don and Lynne, Joe, Greg, and Geoff Herbach – for all of the little things.

CHAPTER ONE: London, July 23, 1825

Samuel Brown bought the house on Wilmont Street because of the large lead glass greenhouse attached to the southern side, but without the intent of ever growing anything. The builder and original owner of the house, who was now dead thirty-some-odd-years and from who Samuel Brown had bought in the twilight of his years, had let the greenhouse fall into disrepair once he was unable to tend to it properly. Large urns of dead flowers and dusty shelves, like miniature fields of uncut hay, had filled it at the time of purchase and most of it now sat next to the carriage house in the same state it had been found, although now the plants were as much as dust themselves. Thirty years of smoke and smog, from both inside and out, collected on the lead glass panes and as the afternoon sun worked to penetrate the film, cast a golden amber hue on the current contents of the greenhouse and its two occupants.

Samuel Brown, engineer by trade and passion, husband and father by luck and passion, and grandfather by the grace of God, sat at his workbench tooling a cooper gasket ring while beneath him, Samuel Brown III ("Sam" to everyone else) worked in the studious manner only three-year-olds on the verge of turning four can, at fixing his wooden train.

"How are the repairs coming, Sam?" Samuel asked, blowing the shavings from the gasket, the white tufts of his hair sticking out around the bands of his magnifying goggles, making him owl-like in appearance.

"Gonna fix good," replied Sam, then blew on his train in imitation of his grandfather, his own auburn hair sticking out around an extra pair of goggles his grandfather had given him, making him, too, near equally as owlish.

"That's good to hear. Ut! Can't have the young princess's breakfast running behind schedule. No, no, no. What was she having again?"

"Auk eggs."

"Ah, yes. Auk eggs hauled in special from the North Pole, I'd imagine. And what else?"

"Polar bear." (Sam pronounced it, of course, as *porar* bear, instigating a small chuckle from the elder Brown.)

"Yes. Polar bear steaks and auk eggs. Mm. Truly a breakfast fit for a princess! Mint sauce for polar bear?"

"Nope."

"No mint sauce? Well, she is our possible future heiress presumptive, but I would want mint sauce for my polar bear, oh, yes, rather much, indeed." Samuel stood up from his chair, leaning over to show his grandson what he had been working on. "Look here, Sam. Your grandfather has finished another piece. Do you wish to help me install it?"

Sam cast aside his train and wood mallet, along with the princess's breakfast that would now be as delayed as everyone else's goods (God bless the royal rail) and ran to the work table dominating the center of the greenhouse, the top of which sat the work of the last eleven years of the elder Samuel Brown's life.

"Careful now, Sam." Samuel lifted his grandson to sit on the table. "It's not running yet, so there's no need to be racing about like it needs catching, oh, no sir, no sir, indeed. Let's see here. Today I finished the gasket for mounting what I am calling the fuel-air mixer. What do you think of that name? Grand, eh?"

Samuel shrugged his shoulders in a very three-year-old going on four fashion.

"Well, I say, when you build your own combustion engine, you can name it what you want. Do you remember where it goes?"

"There?'" Sam asked, pointing to an upper side of the poured steel casement and its attachments that were now the combined sized of a full grown pig.

"Correct! You are most definitely my grandson. Which raises the question of your father. Takes too much after your grandmother, I'm afraid. I'm not sure he knows the working end of a wrench, but he can tell you what is in fashion in the parlors of Paris, much good it does a man." Samuel removed his kerchief to wipe his brow. "I'm sorry, Sam. I should not speak so ill of your father. He . . . he just wasn't what I wished for him, is all."

"Put on now?" Sam's opened eyed expression showed no weight from his grandfather's words.

"That's the show. Onward and upward, Sam. By all means, let's."

As Sam and Samuel leaned over and began lining up boltholes, there was a sharp knock at the greenhouse door. A knock, which Samuel found highly particular, because the rear gate was locked and anyone wishing to get to the greenhouse door would have to walk past the front door to get to it. Both could see the hazy outline of a man and Sam reached for his grandfather's shoulder at the sight of a shadow that stood a head above the top of the greenhouse door, which was fit for a man to walk through without solidly striking his head.

"My, this is interesting," Samuel said, moving to answer the door, but found Sam had a firm hold of his waist coat. "Nothing to be afraid of, Sammy." (It was common practice to call him Sammy when he was distressed.) "Just a man at the door. Why don't you fetch your train and see if you can't get that breakfast back on schedule, eh?"

Samuel lifted his grandson down and watched him scurry beneath the workbench. When Samuel Brown opened the door, he momentarily entertained the thought of joining his grandson under said workbench. The man at the door was seven foot if an inch with the length of him, rail thin, and covered from boot to crown in black save for the part of his face above the ridge of his nose and below his brow. A scarf covered the lower part of his face and a wide brimmed hat, like the type he had seen Spanish priests wearing when he had been part of the Queen's own navy so many years ago, covered his head. The man took Samuel's silence as an invitation and, ducking his head, stepped into the greenhouse.

"Forgive my appearance." The man's voice had a metallic quality, like someone speaking through a length of tin stovepipe. "It is more necessity than theatrics, I assure you. I wish to speak with you, Mr. Brown."

"I'm afraid you have me at a loss, Mister . . . ?"

"Black would be fine," the man said, tipping his head slightly, crossing into the room proper. As he walked, Samuel heard a distinct clicking accompanying each long stride.

"Mr. Black, I'm not sure what I can assist you with, but this is all rather unconventional. One normally notifies a host with the intent to pay a visit and at that, calls to the front door."

"You are correct, Mr. Brown. One normally does. But I, like your invention here, am unconventional."

Samuel's uneasiness at the stranger's appearance was overcome by the revelation that he was aware of what was sitting on his workbench, crossing to where the scarecrow of a gentleman traced the edge of one of the combustion chambers with a gloved finger.

"It is a thing of beauty," Mr. Black said, a touch of wistfulness in his voice. "You should be very, very proud of what you have accomplished. Truly."

"You are an engineer, eh?" Samuel asked. Underneath the workbench, Sam peeked out from where he had squeezed himself behind a crate of scrap metals.

"By necessity," Mr. Black answered without looking up from the engine. "By necessity." His voice dropped. "So very wondrous."

"You are trying my patience, Mr. Black. I'm afraid I must ask your business or ask you to leave."

"Of course, of course. I apologize and I'm afraid I may give you another shock, but it will save us so much time if I just show you." Mr. Black unwound the scarf from his face and beneath was the reason for the metallic quality to his voice: His nose and lower jaw were covered, or, rather, replaced, by bronze fittings. Instead of an opening mouth, Mr. Black had a slotted grill through which could be seen the hint of teeth, sparkling like a white flame.

"Remarkable," Samuel said in an awed voice.

"Not a word I would use," Mr. Black replied, working at unfastening his jacket buttons, doing so slow and precise with stiff fingers. When he opened his jacket, he revealed a cotton undershirt and trousers that had been cut off from just above the knee. The parts of him not covered by clothing, however, were made of metal. From just below his knees, Samuel saw steel rods enclosing a heavy spring with clock works along a toothed rail.

"I saw you hearing my legs," said Mr. Black.

Samuel leaned in closer before checking himself. "I'm sorry. Do you mind?"

"Be my guest."

"Accumulators?" asked Samuel, indicating the spring and gears.

"Yes. Not many men would realize that at first glance. You have a rare talent."

"How many steps?"

"A hundred and seven to fully compress."

"And how high?"

"Standing still I can clear half again the height of a man. At a run, half that again."

"Fascinating." Samuel moved to look from another angle. "The release is in your heels, then?"

"Yes. I call them my spring heels." Mr. Black let the coat fall from his shoulders, revealing the length of his arms. "And these are what I have for trying to do everything else with." From below the elbow, Mr. Black's arms were bronze encasements with wire, pulleys, and springs stretched across them, his hands a clumsy approximation. "Not nearly as useful as the legs. I think the human hand may be perhaps too difficult to replicate, I'm afraid. At least for myself."

"Absolutely fascinating," said Samuel.

"I hoped you could appreciate my work."

"An accident?"

"Dry leprosy."

"Which explains the nose and jaw," said Samuel as an intuitive leap before realizing the callous manner in which he said it. "Oh, dear, I'm dreadfully sorry."

Mr. Black raised a hand. "No need. I've come to accept my condition," he replied, replacing his clothes.

"I'm afraid I don't know how much help I could be. The work you've done so far surpasses my own works in kinetic mechanics."

"Thank you for the offer," Mr. Black said working the buttons again in a deliberate slow and precise manner before looking straight into Samuel's eyes. "But I'm not here about what I've done. I admit, I thought showing you would help you understand that you and I are alike in our nature and I know how difficult what I am going to ask you to do will be."

"I'm not sure I quite follow," said Samuel.

"And part of it was vanity," continued Mr. Black as if not hearing Samuel's interjection. "I think there are very few people who could look upon me with genuine interest and not disgust. Sometimes I fancy showing myself to people." Mr. Black looked up, staring blankly through a pane of the smoked greenhouse glass at the muted shape of the sun. "Showing myself to those pretty young creatures that pay me no mind and hoping one of them doesn't scream. Hoping one of them says, 'My, what a remarkable thing you have become, Jack.' Some day, perhaps. Yes, some day. Hrm."

Mr. Black was lost to himself for a moment before turning sharp and taking up his scarf, wrapping it quickly about his head, as if suddenly embarrassed about his appearance.

"What is it exactly that you want from me, Mr. Black?"

With scarf in place and his voice now again metallic and muffled, Mr. Black said, "You need to stop your work. You need to forget about your combustion engine."

"What? What are you talking about?"

"I work for a select group of people who have a plan for England. A master plan that most certainly does not include a combustion engine of any kind, I'm afraid. I am here as a representative of that same said group."

"This is ridiculous," said Samuel, visibly upset at the unpleasant turn of the conversation. "I wish you to leave. Now." Samuel moved to open the greenhouse door, but was stopped by a firm hand on his shoulder. The hand squeezed steadily and when Samuel started to turn to confront Mr. Black, he saw thin blades had cut their way through the fingertips of the gloves, and, if Mr. Black had wished, he could curl his fingers and ribbon the flesh of Samuel's shoulder. Slowly the pressure released, the blades withdrawing into the cut fabric of the gloves. Samuel turned slowly, giving Mr. Black his full attention.

"Are you going to kill me, then, is that it?"

"No," Mr. Black replied. "But you need to understand the full length the men I work for will go to get what they want. They told me to do whatever it took, but your engine must never see the light of day. Never. You need to think about your family and the consequences of your actions." Mr. Black watched for understanding on Samuel's face, an understanding that "any lengths" included the lives of everyone dear to him. "I told you the two of us are alike. Both of us have accomplished incredible things. Incredible things that no one will ever see."

"You have my word," said Samuel, clearly and without emotion. "I shan't touch it again. Is that good enough?"

"Yes," said Mr. Black as he opened the greenhouse door. "I do wish we could have met under different circumstances. You are a brilliant man, Mr. Samuel Brown. I will make sure you are handsomely compensated for your trouble, you have my word. Perhaps instead, now you could look at advancing steam technology, I hear it is going to be all the rage." He paused, giving the engine one last admiring look. "Good-bye."

Mr. Black closed the greenhouse door and was gone.

Standing for a moment, then slowly at first, and then in a great panic, Samuel threw aside his stool, crawling under the work bench to find where Sam had fallen asleep wedged between the wall and a crate, his small wooden train resting safely on his lap.

Samuel let his grandson sleep while he fetched tarps and other supplies from the carriage house.

CHAPTER TWO: London, July 23, 1894

"Vacuum is the key, Victoria," said Samuel Brown. "Vacuum is the key. A strong lack of pressure that will work as an opposing force, collapsing the chambers before firing again." He worked a see-sawing arm and a pair of attached rods pushed and pulled fitted cylinders. "And your water cooled housing, oho, will ensure that you shan't overheat. Your combustion chambers will control the gas flame and drive the pistons, turning the drive shaft, creating motion from kerosene, not steam." He wiped his slick forehead with the back of his sleeve, leaving a trail of black grease for his efforts. "Of course, you know this already. You were born to do it. And now, rediscovered and modified, you are going to be brilliant, Victoria, brilliant! You will change the world. All you have to do today, though, is show Mr. Quincy your potential." Delighted, he began to pace. "I've been thinking about the velocity problem. Oh, yes. What if we built multiple gear wheels that increased in radius as we increased in momentum? Of course we would need something that could differentiate between the gears. One solution to create a new problem. He spins a tool around his fingers before putting into his apron. He then removed the tool and spun it again.

"Centrifugal force? Mhmmm . . . . Centrifugal force! As the drive spins faster, the force would push outwards – to the larger gears. By Jove, Victoria, you are brilliant! Brilliant!"

"Ahem."

She had snuck up upon him again. He sighed and let his shoulder drop. "Oh, sorry, a bit too loud again, Miss O'Brien?" Samuel made a mental note to either place a lock on the door that led from the house proper to his greenhouse-prior-workshop, or possibly outfit her with a nice jangly bell around her neck.

"Mm, a touch," replied his housekeeper, a rather fetching and pleasingly proportioned young red haired woman carrying a tea service with two cups. "Talkin' to it again are you, Mr. Brown? You're lucky the Bobbies don't hear you a-carrying on as such. Likely to throw you in the nut hatch as look kindly on what you keep hidden under that sheet."

Samuel sighed. "Her name is 'Victoria,' Miss O'Brien. In honor of our Queen regnant of the United Kingdom of Great Britain and Ireland and the first Empress of India of the British Raj and her many fruitful years on the throne."

"And my cat may be named Bonnie Prince, but you won't find me chewin' the fat with him."

Samuel smiled, although she tried her best to suppress it, Miss O'Brien's Irish brogue still managed to peek out a bit whenever they were alone together, pleasing him greatly. "Miss O'Brien, I don't believe there is another house keeper in all of London that possesses the extremely frank disposition that you do. In all probability, they would have been terminated the instant they scolded the master of the house for his stockings possessing, what had you called it? A right stink to them that would turn the stomach of ol' Scratch himself."

"And it's a good thing that you could find an able bodied person such as myself that's willing to put up with such a stench. Huh! Not only that, but to cook your meals and clean your house and keep a keen eye on the day to day activities that you seem so willing to overlook while you're out here talking to your precious Victoria."

"Is that jealousy I hear?" Samuel chuckled, stepping in closer to her. "You'll have to forgive me, but I was still focused on you able bodied." He attempted to kiss her.

"Samuel!"

"Shannon!"

She stepped back, keeping him at arm's length. "Ut! 'Miss O'Brien,' if you please. I am on duty and I will not have you stealing kisses with company due. The sun is up for goodness sakes."

Samuel smiled, over dramatically placing his hands at his hips. "Then stop being stubborn and say 'yes.'"

"I will not. It's not proper. You are a man of means. You come from a good and proper family and . . . I do not. It's not proper. Not right."

"That doesn't matter. I am in love with you, Shan— er, Miss O'Brien."

She folded her arms. "It does matter. Proper is proper."

Samuel stepped forward. "Well, it shouldn't and it won't. Not anymore. It's a new world happening out there, my dear. You can smell it in the air. Such wondrous, wondrous things." Samuel began to pace, his excitement growing with every step.

"Did you know that the Germans have created a device that works like the telephone, but without wires? Imagine, talking to someone in another country while standing outside, or, my God, on a boat. There's a rumor that a Frenchman has invented a typewriter that types for itself. You just tell it what you want written and it does all the rest. Don't you see? A new world is being born all around us and I am doing my part. My combustion engine, I don't know, maybe one day people will have horse carriages but without the horse. Who knows? But my point is that—What was yesterday, won't matter a whit tomorrow. The idea of society deciding who can love one another will make no more difference than . . . than an antiquated steam engine will to my Victoria."

Stopping by his workbench, Samuel crossed his arms. "Very well, you leave me no choice. Unless you agree to marry me I will hold my breath until the vapors leave my body."

Miss O'Brien shook her head.

"No? All right, then." Samuel sucked in a deep breath, holding it.

Miss O'Brien pretended not to care, even so far as to begin dusting a nearby table.

Samuel collapsed, dramatically, and then stop-ped moving altogether.

"You're not a funny man, Mr. Samuel Brown IV. A fit and proper gentleman would not treat a lady such. You just be getting yourself up and tend-ing to your business before your company gets here and finds you lyin' about. Mr. Brown? Samuel? It's not funny, Samuel. Samuel?" Shannon ceased her dusting and now stood over him. "Fine. Fine, I'll have ya. Just stop your foolin'."

Samuel's eyes fluttered open, followed by a wink.

"Oh!" And with that she kicked him.

"Ow!"

"You're a cruel man and I would not have such traits in a man I call husband."

Samuel bounded up, brushing himself off. "You're absolutely right. I hereby, from this mo-ment forward, may the Lord strike me dead if I lie, swear off faking my own death."

"You shall not be taking the Lord's name in vain in *my* home." Miss O'Brien stopped, realizing what she had just said, along with the enormity of it all.

Samuel smiled, triumphant at last.

"All right, then," she said.

"Yes?" Samuel stepped forward, clasping her hands.

"Yes."

"Oho! You have made me a very happy man, Shannon." Again he tried to lean in and steal a kiss, and again she retreated at arm's length.

"Ahem, 'Miss O'Brien.'"

"Right, right." Samuel took a step back. "Ahem. And aren't you forgetting something?" She showed him her ring finger.

"You're right. You're absolutely right." Samuel immediately began rummaging about his workshop, tossing aside odd bits and pieces, until, finally . . .

"Aha, here!" He had collected a coil of copper wire for the band.

"Well, that is a start, I suppose," teased Miss O'Brien.

"Well, then." Samuel then set upon finding something small and shiny. "And this." He produced a piece of crystal, and with a nod of approval from his beloved, set upon the task crafting a modest, yet suitable token of his love and affection. Soon thereafter, he turned to Miss O'Brien, took to knee, and held out his quickly constructed engagement ring.

"Ahem, Miss Shannon O'Brien, will you take this simple inventor to be—"

"Yes!" And she kissed him twice as he lifted her up and spun her around.

There was a knock at the door to the outside.

Miss O'Brien immediately brushed down her uniform and moved to open the door.

Samuel grabbed her playfully around the waist.

"Mr. Brown!" she cried, protesting, playfully swatting at him.

"Future *Mrs.* Brown," reminded Samuel.

Smiling, she stole another quick kiss, and then opened the door.

An impeccably dressed short gentleman stepped in, a man of high station and education by his strict bearing and demeanor.

"Thomas!" cried Samuel. "Right on time, as always. Even when five minutes late would be even better."

The man named Thomas screwed up his face in puzzlement. "I'm sorry?"

"Nothing. Mr. Thomas Quincy, allow me to introduce my house keeper and future—"

"Would you care for a spot of tea, Mr. Quincy?" asked Miss O'Brien, interjecting politely.

"Not the most proper, is she?" Thomas stepped further in to the room, his back now to his hosts. "I think that's true of all the Irish. Poor manners all around. It's in their blood."

Samuel started to defend Miss O'Brien, but she stopped him with a shake of her head.

"So, tell me, Samuel," continued Thomas, "what is so important that I had to see it for my own eyes? Hm? Have you invented your automatic bread toaster you talked of in university? Or maybe the machine to look through people? Always good for a laugh."

"Not through people, Thomas," said Samuel. "Into. To look inside of a person without having to cut them open. To see the body operate while still alive. Think of the lives it could save."

"I say, invent something to keep people from getting sick in the first place, then you'd be on to something. While you're at it, invent something to give the Irish manners." Thomas turned, noting Miss O'Brien was still in the room. "Oh, I'm sorry. No tea for me, thank you."

Miss O'Brien curtsied, and left.

"See? No manners," concluded Thomas. "A good English servant would have said, 'As you wish.'"

"I see your life after university has done nothing for softening your disposition. Once a blaggard, always a blaggard."

"Pffft, don't be such a soft heart, Samuel. It was you that almost begged me to come down here and see what you've been tinkering with. I don't have time to waste with the work load I carry at the ministry, and if it wasn't for the fact we were school chums once I wouldn't be here at all and you would do well to remember that."

"Yes. You're right. Thank you for making the time to pay me a visit and I promise to make it worth your while. The reason I called you was I have been working on something that I believe—"

"Do you have any Scotch out here in your laboratory, Dr. Frankenstein?" Thomas interrupted.

"I'm sorry?"

"Have you read it then?"

"Well, yes, I—"

"Frightfully good read. Word in the social circles is it based upon actual happenings, did you know that?"

"Um . . . no, no I did not."

Thomas slid a finger along the workbench. "They say the monster was spotted by an expedition to find the North Pole just last summer."

"After all these years?"

"So they say."

"'They?'"

"My sources in the more secret circles of government, my good man. Very hush-hush, if you catch my full meaning."

"Oh."

There was a long pause as Thomas continued inspecting the workshop.

"I could have Miss O'Brien bring you some," said Samuel, finally.

"That's all right. I've brought my own." Thomas pulled a small flask from his pocket. "Wouldn't want a potato eater to handle my drink, anyway." At that he took a strong swig, returning the flask immediately to his pocket. "So, are you going to show me this invention of yours or not? You asked for the ministry to have a look and the ministry is now here."

"Yes. Of course." Samuel pulled the sheet off the table revealing his engine. "I call her 'Victoria.'"

Thomas smiled. "Very patriotic. I like it already. Now, then, what does it do?"

"It is a water cooled, gas vacuum, kerosene combustion engine," said Samuel with pride.

The smile disappeared. "I see."

"Do you?" said Samuel, trying to hide his excitement. "Do you know what this means?"

"Maybe you should tell me, Samuel," said Thomas, coolly.

"How much coal do you think there is in England?" Seeing no reaction, Samuel immediately continued. "In the world?"

Thomas gave a small shrug in response, still unsmiling.

"There are already rumors of mines running dry in the north and in the meantime we are building more steam boilers for everything from ocean liners and trains to . . . to . . . flying machines."

Still no response of any kind from Thomas. Samuel was getting a bit worried. "I just read that a pair of Americans are working on a steam rocket with hopes of touching the moon. Can you imagine that? All the way to the moon. My point is: We have a new found need for mechanical power and I believe it will only continue to grow and become more and more sophisticated. Who knows . . . two hundred years from now, everyone could own their own powered mechanical flying carriage." Samuel began to pace. "But what happens if we run out of coal? There has to be a finite amount right? (Oh, and don't even get me started on the practical uses of land conservation.) We'll need an alternate power source and I have found that source. We have a near endless supply, so much so that we burn it to light our streets at night because it's cheaper than wood."

Thomas finally stirred. "Kerosene." The word almost sounded alien coming from Thomas's lips.

"That's right," continued Samuel, now a bit relieved. "A kerosene engine that's simpler and more efficient." He pointed at his invention. "Look. No boiler. No fire box. No coal hopper. The fire takes place in four separate combustion chambers and the force is directly applied to pistons that in turn crank the drive. See? No energy is wasted. No more smog, no more such ghastly unhealthy air. No more risk of everything getting shut down until the air cleared. It will change everything."

"And if I asked you to destroy it?" said Thomas, a bit too quickly.

"What? Did I hear you correctly? Destroy it?"

"Yes."

Samuel waited for an explanation, yet received none. "Why? Th-that's ridiculous. Why would I destroy it?" Samuel paused. "Ah, now I see. You're kidding me again. Like at university. Thomas, always the jokester."

Thomas took a few steps, inspecting his fingernails. "No joke, Samuel. I am asking you to destroy it."

"What? What is this about, Thomas? What aren't you telling me?"

"Because we were once school chums I will tell you what I can, and then I will ask one last time." He made sure this time that Samuel was able to look him in the eye. "After that it is out of my hands. Utterly and completely. Do you understand, Samuel?"

"You're not making sense, Thomas."

"Am I?"

"You're being foolish."

"England has invested her future, socially and politically, in steam. There are factories right now, as we speak, building the boilers and pressure lines and check valves that will bring a Golden Age to England. Those factories didn't just magically appear overnight, you know. Men – hard working men – invested their time and money in the building of those factories with the promise, a promise by England herself, that it was money well invested. Now, what if someone were to come along and say that the future is not steam? That the future is in fact kerosene? England would have egg on her face, wouldn't she? And those men – the men that built those factories to make those boilers and pressure lines and check values – well, they'd be caught with their hand up the skirt of a tart with egg on her face and the fact of the matter is, they pay me very well to make sure that isn't the case."

"Thomas . . ." Samuel did not like the glint in Thomas's narrowing eyes.

Thomas stepped in closer, now within arm's reach. "Now I told you I was going to ask you one last time to destroy it, but I can see by the look on your face that it would be a waste of my breath to try.

"I—"

"I would like to tell you that you've put me in a difficult, awkward position, but because we were school chums I'm going to do you two favors. First, I'm not going to lie to you. You're *not* putting me in a difficult position, because I like what I do. I'm good at what I do. I truly am. Before being approached by my current employers – not the ministry, mind you, but my *real* employers – I was plying my trade down White Chapel way a few years back. They recognized I had a talent, but said I was wasting it playing in the gutters. Irish whores are a soft spot for me, you know."

Samuel gasped, stepping back, now realizing with whom he was truly dealing with, and it chilled him to the marrow. "You . . . you're . . .?"

Thomas smiled, fiendishly. "Yes. I am. Or, rather, I was."

"Dear God in heaven."

Thomas stepped in again. "Which brings me to my second favor: I won't touch *your* Irish whore."

"My . . . ?" A small bead of sweat ran down Samuel's face.

Thomas leaned in, still smiling. "We know. We've been watching you for a while. I told them you were a dreamer and you have to watch out for the dreamers. They don't pay attention to the bottom line. Night-night, Sammy, my boy."

Thomas flicked a knife from his coat sleeve, and, with one deft move, stabbed Samuel clean through the heart.

"Hurrgggkkk!" Samuel clutched at his chest in disbelief, his life force quickly ebbed.

"Don't let them bed bugs bite." Thomas started whistling a happy tune, exiting through the city door outside as Samuel collapsed in a heap.

A short time passed before Miss O'Brien returned from the house proper.

"I heard the door, Samuel. Is he gone then? Dreadful man. Your school chum has the manner of a longshoreman. Samuel?" She gazed down at his motionless form on the floor, and sighed. "I already said 'yes.' Get yourself off the floor, you'll catch chill taking naps like that and I'll not be spending my time tending house and nursing you back to health." His not stirring made her uneasy, so she stamped her foot. "Samuel Brown! I find absolutely no humor in this. Stop this instance." She crossed over to him, trembling. "You promised. You promised. I am to be your wife and you promised not to be cruel to me. Oh, Samuel. You promised." She dropped to her knees beside him.

A passing bobby rushed to her aid when the screaming started as she saw the pooling blood.

CHAPTER THREE: The Game Is Afoot

The two men entered the Brown residence two days later from the door leading into the alley, the one that directly lead into the recently deceased's work room, the first to enter being a noted inspector from Scotland Yard, a particular dresser barely the five-feet, seven-inches reacquired to qualify at the start of his profession and an equally noted medical man, more well known as a highly prized assistant than as physician in most London-based social and literary circles.

"Here you go, Dr. Watson, the scene of the murder," said the shorter, sallow, rat-faced man.

"Thank you, Lestrade," replied the famed assistant and biographer.

"Hm." The inspector's dark eyes narrowed.

Dr. Watson cocked his head at the inspector. "I say, you've kept mostly to yourself this entire time, no callously brushing me off, nor a single condescending comment about me or—"

"Speaking of whom, where is he?" said Lestrade, slyly trying to hide the annoyance in his voice the very best he could.

"Said he needed to check a few things out on his own, he did, said he'd meet us here shortly," replied Dr. Watson, eying him suspiciously.

"Hm."

"See, right there." Dr. Watson nearly jabbed the poor fellow with his accusing finger.

"What?" asked Inspector Lestrade.

"We know it irks you to no end when he does this, and you never spare us in the telling so."

Lestrade stepped in place, still trying very hard not to seem rankled or annoyed. "Look, Scotland Yard's orders are to assist at the best of our ability, *especially* where *he* is concerned, and that means—"

"By whose authority?" pressed Dr. Watson, arching his eyebrows.

"The highest, save the Queen's and the PM's," said Lestrade, quickly deflecting the question.

"Then . . . ?"

Lestrade held up his hand. "Ut! I've already said enough. Now, if you'd kindly excuse me, Dr. Watson . . . ?" He turned for the door.

"Hmp. By all means, then."

"Good." And Inspector Lestarde quickly exited the way he came.

Dr. Watson stepped further into the room, poked a bit at a bookshelf and some of the scattered about equipment, and then stopped. "I presume you heard well enough, then?" he called out after a brief pause.

Sherlock Holmes, the famed detective, entered the room from the other door, keeping his profile low before turning slow, revealing the brass mech-anic that covered a third of his face, skull, and left eye – his left arm stiff and gloved, the end results of a harrowing life-threatening incident a few years prior.

"Yes, Watson, I did. Thank you, that was most, dare I say, enlightening."

"Then, do you suppose . . . ?"

"Oh, yes, as I suspected, my dear brother is clearly directly involved in this entire tawdry affair."

"Hm. That most definitely adds a new wrinkle to all of this, surely."

"Oh, yes. Quite."

"Well." Dr. Watson quickly changed the subject. "It appears finding where Mr. Brown was killed will prove obvious."

"It has been my experience, Watson, the 'what,' 'where,' and 'when' are the simplest of the five to deduce. Of course there are exceptions to every rule, take the murder of that one particular gentleman a year ago."

"You mean that writer fellow, Haggard," said Dr. Watson.

"Correct. Mr. H. Rider Haggard." Holmes shook his head, sighing at the tragedy of it all. "Apparently drowned in the Thames, but with no water in his lungs and almost every bone in his body having been shattered." Holmes began to pace about the workshop, investigating.

"Yes. Conventional wisdom said that he was beaten to death and then thrown in the river, but you noted, Holmes, there was no bruising, and thus, the breaking of the bones must have taken place simultaneously at the instant of his death or afterward which would have left open the cause of death. In that case we knew only the 'what' – a young writer of some promise had been seen in the company of known street urchins and their handler."

"Dodger."

"Ah, yes, the Artful Dodger. Dreadful little man. Heh. When you clobbered him with your walking stick when he tried to pinch your wallet . . ."

Holmes allowed himself a slight smile. "Yes."

Dr. Watson chuckled. "Haggard was doing research for the sequel to his still current best seller and suddenly turns up in the river, dead with no link to Dodger except being seen in his company earlier. Until you put your considerable talents to it, Holmes. To realize he had been thrown from the Kaiser's visiting zeppelin. A zeppelin! The impact against the river from that height like being hit by a locomotive."

"A mere, simple matter of deduction, Watson, really."

"Hm. Simple to you, perhaps, but for the rest of us, quite an entirely different matter, I assure you." Dr. Watson began to lose himself in thought.

Holmes stopped his reminiscing, noticing his friend's peculiar look. "What, Watson?"

"Oh, Haggard's silly book. *She Who Must Be Obeyed*. Poppycock. I don't care if some do claim that it could be true. Pure flights of fancy, I say."

"Like clockwork men, Watson?" Holmes smiled again. "How did Shakespeare put it in *Hamlet* if I may so boldly paraphrase?

'There are more things in heaven and earth, Watson,
than are dreamt of in your philosophy.'"

"Yes, well, immortal witch goddesses, lost worlds, pillars of flame, feh!"

"And I am sure we shall encounter even stranger yet in our careers, mark my words, old friend."

"Unfortunately, Holmes, judging from past experiences, I must agree with you . . ."

"And now we come to face the murder of inventor Mr. Samuel Brown. We know the 'where,' here, in his workshop. The 'how?' Stabbed. Let us see if we can discover our remaining answers, shall we? What can we deduce from what we know so far?"

Dr. Watson pulled out his notebook, immediately setting upon the task. "Mr. Brown was stabbed inside his workshop and discovered early morning by the milk service. The payment being due, the man first knocked at the service door, then moved around the house eventually looking through the window of the workshop door, there, and saw the body . . . here."

"Who would normally handle payments?"

"Patience, Holmes." Dr. Watson flipped a page. "The house keeper, Miss O'Brien, would have normally handled such matters, but she herself has sadly vanished. From the preliminary examination of Mr. Brown's body, you will note trace odors of Scotch and perfume."

"Deduction?"

"Pluralitas non est ponenda sine necessitate would lead us to the simplest answer as the correct one," said Dr. Watson, proudly. "Mr. Brown, a bachelor, laboring in his workshop, becomes thirsty and sends Miss O'Brien, described by neighbors as a very attractive young woman employed as his house keeper, for a glass of Scotch. Continuing his work he sends for another drink and then another and so on. Each time he notes the physical qualities of Miss O'Brien. Emboldened, if not possessed by spirits, Mr. Brown begins an unwanted advance on the virtues of Miss O'Brien. Resisting, a struggle ensued. Using a knife from the tea service to defend

herself, she stabs Mr. Brown in the chest and flees, fearing her position and nationality detrimental to her innocence."

"Well done, Watson. You would be a credit to the Yard."

Dr. Watson gave a half sigh, shaking his head. "Ah, this would be the point in which you point out the many deficiencies of my theory."

"Nothing so barbaric, Watson. Your analytical construction was both solid and supported."

"And yet?"

"Occam's crumpet."

"Occam's . . . *crumpet*? Are you being serious, Holmes?"

"Quite, although, by your reasoning, I prefer *entia non sunt multiplicanda praeter necessitate* as modified by our present situation, hence . . ."

"Very well. What would this unheard of *crumpet* principle have us believe?"

"Simply this: 'Anything involving Mother England is a landscape of holes and crevices.'"

"Ah, so you believe a conspiracy is afoot."

Holmes nodded. "Indeed."

"That England herself is working against us in this matter," continued Dr. Watson.

"Not against, Watson, but it is my firm belief that she is actively protecting her interests, whatever they may be, in this sordid matter. These are wondrous and dark times, Watson. Wondrous and dark. Let us look to the things that suggest there was more than common red nosed debauchery at work here." Holmes began to poke about the premises once more.

Dr. Watson paused before speaking again, watching his friend go to work on the case.

"There has been a turn to your demeanor, Holmes."

"Mm."

Dr. Watson shifted his weight, a bit like a little boy who had to admit he had had his hands in the cookie jar. "Ever since— after— I'm not sure I care for it much, and I am ashamed to say it gives me more than a slight sense of unease around you."

Holmes looked down, paused, and then readdressed his friend. "Have I told you that I find my arm itches in the night? I wake with the urge to scratch, but my fingers find only an empty space. Then I sense it." Holmes glanced at his artificial arm. "The clockwork limb that has become its replacement sitting in the darkness, across the room, waiting for the dawn and for me to fumble with its straps and gears – reminiscent of the ministrations I once gave that accursed violin I can no longer play. Then I open the iris of my new eye and the darkness is pierced. I look upon the arm and wonder if it is dreaming of a body that itches." Holmes paused. "I need Scotch."

"Pardon?"

"Scotch, Watson, I need Scotch."

"I am not one to tell another gentleman his matters, as you well know, but I don't believe succor will be found in drink."

Holmes smiled wryly. "The Scotch, Watson. Bring the whole decanter and, while in the house, if you could fetch the diary of Miss O'Brien. An educated guess would place it under the pillow of her bed. Trust in me, Watson."

"Of course, Holmes." Dr. Watson left the detective to his own musings and went further into the house to fetch the items requested.

Holmes watched the door close behind Dr. Watson, listened to the sound of his heavy, confident stride down the hall, and then let out a sigh that lowered his shoulders, causing the strapping of his arm to pinch. Something he may have Dr. Jekyll look at, but sooner rather than later, his intuition told him that the nervous doctor was becoming a fluid element, unsure and inconstant, a condition that Holmes found undesirable at best. Hesiod, a Greek of pious disposition, had called it Chaos and Holmes found it to be a constant thorn in the side of rational deduction.

Holmes rubbed the pinch and worked a finger under the leather strap. It was something he tried not to do in front of Dr. Watson. Although he would never state as much, anything that highlighted the changes in Holmes' corpus was an added weight to Dr. Watson's soul. In the time since Reichenbach, his rehabilitation had been a trial for Dr. Watson. He never doubted Dr. Watson's friendship, but there had been an increasing number of times where Homes had seen in Dr. Watson's eyes that he was beginning to doubt himself and it troubled Holmes that he could find no way to reassure him. Dr. Watson would always be the most perfect companion a gentleman could ask for and therein lay the dilemma. Dr. Watson would swear on his deathbed that Holmes was nothing but a man's man, but Holmes himself had now become unsure. What made a gentleman? Surely a veteran, returning from the horrors of war, having lost limbs to man's incredible aptitude for death and maiming, having left a gentleman is no less a one upon his return. The count of limbs does not a good soul make. It had been something else, something left at the bottom of that watery drop that caused Holmes to doubt the status of his character and for all his deductive abilities, he could not discover what. He sighed again, this time cursing the offending leather strap.

That being neither here nor there, Holmes closed his eyes, turned to the room with his back to the house door and opened his remaining senses. An exercise in focus practiced by various Swamis and Buddhists, Holmes measured his heart rate and controlled his breath, first turning inward and then without.

Although the boiler was not fired, forcing steam throughout the rooming works, there was no drip of escaping water from the copper piping that was common in shoddy fittings and improper maintenance. Samuel Brown was precise *and* studious.

There was no rattle to the glass panes of the greenhouse even with the gusts that marked

London's predictable climate this time of year. With their age, it was apparent that someone competently replaced the mounting putty. Holmes was confident Samuel Brown had been that someone. He cared for the things in his possession.

The room was filled with the smell of kerosene, but under that were other stray scents. Pipe smoke, an Indian blend was predominant, common enough from the East India Trading Company, but there was another wafting there. Sharper to the nose, something distinctly American. Samuel Brown was both conventional and experimental. With the smell of tobacco was also the acrid smell of blood. Then grease. Cleaners. Wood smoke. Leather. Perfume.

He opened his eyes. Inspecting the dried blood pool, he noted the size and shape taking into account the position of the body according to the police report. Samuel Brown had been facing the outside door. Holmes's mind ran through the probable scenarios, placing his attacker between the two, preventing escape and providing egress, a thoughtful killer or a practiced one. Brown was closer to the house door than the protection of the table, something he could have put between him and his attacker if he had been aware of an oncoming assault. Perhaps he had been attempting to flee the house or protect something, or someone, inside?

Around the room, each tool and instrument was neatly in its home. Nothing disturbed. Tea service, untouched, apparently placed hastily by Ms. O'Brien. Plain biscuits without preserves. She didn't like the guest. If only Samuel Brown had sensed what Ms. O'Brien apparently instinctively knew. Unless a common familiarity had blinded him to any danger.

Holmes strode to the table that dominated the center of the room, gazing at Mr. Brown's creation. Fascinating. Holmes understood the concepts; saw the mechanics, but even then, the meticulous work-manship, the magnitude of its creation impressed him to no end. Samuel Brown was indeed a gifted creator and half hidden under his creation's cover-ings was apparently his notes. Holmes pulled the leather bound book from under the canvas, opening the cover. Old. Much older than Samuel Brown himself. Odd. Flipping through pages, noting the yellowing effect age had taken to pages exposed to sunlight most often, he was almost half through when needed to return to the beginning to verify something he had already suspected.

"Galapagos," Holmes said with a thin smile on his lips. Flipping through the remaining pages, he set the book back on the table and pulled out his pocket watch. Moving the minute hand slightly to what his body told him was the correct time; he listened for Dr. Watson's return and was rewarded with his footfalls only half a minute after his estimated arrival.

"Hm. It appears that Mr. Brown had also developed an itch of sorts." Holmes checked his watch as Dr. Watson returned from within the house proper carrying a full decanter of brown liquid along with a small book with a ribbon protruding out of it to mark a page.

"Correct again, Holmes," said Dr. Watson, waving the small book.

"Excellent, Watson," complimented Holmes. "Now let us inebriate ourselves and delve into a woman's pool of secret wishes."

"HOLMES!"

Holmes chuckled. "A blarney, Watson. I merely wished to show you I retain my sense of whimsy even in my current condition."

"You mean I fetched the Scotch and diary for Mr. Tom Foolery?"

"No, Watson, those two items are clues and keys to proving that Mr. Samuel Brown was killed not by the house keeper, but by an adversary we have faced before."

"Oh, really, Holmes? Whom?"

"Evil incarnate, Watson, evil incarnate. We face evil and even more terrible is, if I am correct, it is an evil compounded by evil. All of which hides under the very nose of England."

"Slow down, Holmes. You told me you saw Moriarty's dead broken form at the bottom of the waterfall. That you almost crawled over him as you pulled yourself from the water and certain death."

Homes shook his head. "Not him, Watson. Moriarty has most certainly shook off his mortal coil due to his passing at Reichenbach Falls. No, Watson, this is a criminal most heinous that slipped between my fingers once before, but will not again."

Dr. Watson frowned. "I'm afraid you've lost me, Holmes."

"Not to worry, Watson. Let us examine the clues. First, how much Scotch is left in the bottle?"

Dr. Watson held forth the bottle. "All of it. It's full."

"Meaning?"

"He wasn't drinking from this bottle."

"Or?"

"The house keeper refilled it before she left. Which doesn't make sense."

"Or?"

"Or what, Holmes?"

"Or Mr. Brown picked up the smell of Scotch from somewhere or someone else. Remember, Watson, I said he possessed only the *trace* odor of Scotch. Not that of a man who had spent the day swimming in it. You can set the decanter aside. Now, smell the diary."

Dr. Watson placed the decanter on the work-bench, leaned in, and sniffed the diary, wrinkling his nose at the scent. "Ah. The same perfume as one Miss O'Brien?"

"Correct. Although not proving anything, be-cause of their proximity, but it does point towards what the content of two books will reveal."

"Really? How so?"

"Here's the journal of Mr. Brown. Keep in mind that our victim was an inventor and more importantly, an engineer by trade."

Dr. Watson took the handed journal, paging through it. "What should I be looking for, Holmes? I see notes and sketches and schematics."

"Doodles, Watson. Doodles."

"Doodles, Holmes?"

"If you study the majority of the journal you find the accoutrements of a man fascinated by mathematics, shapes, and the physical world. The journal of an engineer, but look to the last sections of the book, notably the side bars."

Dr. Watson did as told, flipping towards the back. "Are those birds?"

"I took them for fish, but Mr. Brown's artistic ability aside, he had been overcome with fits of fancy. There are other clues in the journal concerning another matter, but I will keep them to myself for the moment."

Dr. Watson sighed. "As you wish, Holmes."

"Now, back to the task at hand: if you will look to the last pages of Miss O'Brien's diary. I am loath to invade the secrets of a woman, but a man is dead. You shall be her confidante, Watson. Tell me only of matters of the heart and I trust anything you read you shall keep your own council on."

"I am a gentleman first and foremost, Mr. Holmes."

"Of course. I apologize, Watson. I didn't mean to question your integrity. I only— it has been— I have not been myself as of late."

Dr. Watson opened a page marked by the ribbon and quickly read what was there. "By Jove, Holmes. Someone had asked her to marry. She loves him, but worries about propriety. No name is given. Heavens, the two of them."

"Does it seem logical that she killed him now? Hardly. And as a footnote, the tea service was a sweet biscuit, requiring no knife. The person that killed Mr. Brown brought the tool with him, showing his intent to do bodily harm. No murder of passion whatsoever."

"But why? Why would someone kill him?"

"Let us handle the 'who' first and I believe the last pieces will become self-evident. Our next piece of the puzzle should be arriving about—" Holmes checked his watch again, smiled, and pointed at the door that led to the outside. "Now."

And, sure enough, there was a knock at that door.

Dr. Watson turned to Holmes, amazed. "How ever did you?"

"Dr. Henry Jekyll is a master of clock works and like his creations, he is nothing if not punctual," said Holmes, matter-of-factly.

Dr. Watson crossed to the door and opened it. There stood an elderly, smartly dressed bespect-acled man holding onto black kit bag whose dour expression could easily curdle milk, if given half the chance.

"Dr. Jekyll. A pleasure to see you again," greet-ed Dr. Watson to the best of his ability.

Dr. Jekyll ignored Dr. Watson, instead marching right up to Holmes, stating his business clearly and to the point: "Mr. Holmes, I have completed the internal inspection of the cadaver and now, as per our agreement, I would have a look at the ongoing workings of my creation."

"I see you were not struck by a trolley carrying etiquette on your way over, Dr. Jekyll," said Dr. Watson, non-plussed with a sniff. "How good to see there are in fact such constant rigid consistencies in our universe."

"Hm," Dr. Jekyll replied.

"What can you tell us of Mr. Brown's condition?" interjected Holmes.

"I assume you refer to the nature of the wound and not in fact the obvious condition of being dead," said Dr. Jekyll. "Remove your jacket, please."

Holmes began to disrobe to reveal his clockwork arm, while Dr. Jekyll opened his bag of tools and delicate instruments. When both had completed their tasks, Dr. Jekyll went about inspecting and tinkering upon the prosthetic device.

"Have you been winding it twice daily?"

Homes nodded.

"Have you preformed the preventative steps I instructed you in?" Dr. Jekyll's tone was nearly indistinguishable from a medical doctor's bedside manner.

"Mr. Holmes is not a school boy, Dr. Jekyll," said Dr. Watson, eyes narrowing.

"I have done everything you have instructed in caring for it," said Holmes, ignoring Dr. Watson. "Now if you could tell us of your findings, there is a man and his fiancée in need of justice and a killer to capture."

"Death by exsanguination. Inflicted by a knife. Double edged. Thin blade. At least six inches long. It entered directly under the sternum, piercing the thoracic cavity." Dr. Jekyll paused, then continued. "It was then pivoted. The motion severed the inferior vena cava and the descending aorta."

"By accident?"

"One doesn't not accidentally sever the body's largest artery and vein without causing undue damage to the surrounding tissue or running afoul of the protection of the rib cage. This wound did neither. Whoever stabbed your victim was a practiced hand that had intimate knowledge of the structure of internal organs. Clean. Effective. And highly skilled. A doctor or possibly a very gifted butcher. Also the positioning and slight angle suggests he is short and right handed."

"Sound familiar, Watson?" called Holmes.

Dr. Watson frowned. "I hope you are not suggesting what I fear you are, Holmes."

"You have not been winding it properly," said Dr. Jekyll with a scowl. "It will only continue to function if you give it the full attention to detail that it demands."

"How can you be so fixated on that blasted contraption?" questioned Dr. Watson. "A gifted man's life has been prematurely extinguished and you continue on about a . . . about a glorified pocket watch."

"Watson," said Holmes, evenly. "What was that you had been saying about telling a gentleman his manners? Hm?"

Dr. Watson gave out a small huff. "Drinking is one thing, but complete disregard for the life and death of a man is something else entirely."

Holmes cracked his neck. "I apologize if Dr. Watson has offended you, Dr. Jekyll. He is both blessed and cursed with an empathy that would be the envy of saints."

"No need," said Dr. Jekyll plainly. "I take his observation on my detachment as a compliment. Where some see a lack of social graces, I see efficiency . . . and salvation. Emotion will not allow your new arm to grasp a cup. Focus and an analytical approach to problem solving allows technology to achieve what was once thought as impossible. To be honest, I envy you, Mr. Holmes. You are closer to the perfection I seek. I believe that we are all of two minds. Two parts of the whole. Imagine what could be accomplished if we could separate the wasteful tendencies – sloth, lust, wrath, and leave only a purity of thought. Imagine what we could accomplish."

"To remove that what makes us human?" asked Dr. Watson with a snort.

"Our definitions of human maybe quite different," continued Dr. Jekyll. "This person, Brown, that you insist I weep over. What is he to you now? Someone to mourn? Still a human being in all but action? To me he is a failed machine that cannot be repaired, but if I am successful in my endeavors, maybe I can change that. If I can remove the shackles of emotion, I open a world of possibility. Surely, if anyone can appreciate what I hope to accomplish it is the notoriously cool and analytical Sherlock Holmes. My earlier . . . ahem . . . attempts only led to folly, as you well know, and if it were not for you and Mr. Stevenson and certain well placed authorities . . ."

"I have nothing but admiration for your drive and dedication and my thanks for what you have done for me, but I cannot help but think concerning your alter ego's prior crimes that you should be more careful what you wish for, my good doctor, you may receive it," replied Holmes.

"True. And therein lies the cosmic rub, indeed, Mr. Holmes. Very well. A good day to you, gentlemen."

"Good day," said Holmes.

And with that the illustrious and formerly quite infamous Dr. Henry Jekyll quickly packed up his bag and went out the door.

"First a death and then his company. Like a chill in the bones," said Dr. Watson after making sure the eccentric inventor was well out of earshot.

"One could say that science is a cruel and jealous mistress," mused Holmes.

"One can also say, 'good riddance.' I still shudder at the particulars of *that* case." There was a long pause before Dr. Watson spoke again. "Did what he say have an attraction for you, Holmes? A pure analytical mind, void of emotion?"

"No, Watson. I enjoy my emotion, dark as it may be at times, these days. Although I may appear aloft and removed, I am much too fond of your company to ever imagine giving it up and the idea of love is a mystery that I will never stop pursuing even given my recent turn of events. But enough of me being a flibbertigibbet, there is a killer on the loose, and as the information provided by our thankfully now good doctor shows, a skilled and knowledgeable one at that."

Dr. Watson lowered his voice. "Do you really believe our murderer could be *him*?"

"Do you remember what I told you when the killings stopped?"

"When you took to reading obituaries for weeks on end? You said that he was someone who couldn't stop themselves. Someone that would keep killing until, how did you put it, was acted upon by an outside force equal or greater than his own."

"Correct, Watson, and since, much to my own embarrassment, I was not that force and it wasn't the constabulary, I believed he may have met an appropriate if unrelated death. Since I believed our killer was an educated man of position, this would have been of note in the paper. I never found a passing that fit our man. I now believe that he was stopped by someone else. Someone that placed him on a different path, but no less criminal and foul."

"But why, Holmes? Why would Jack the Ripper kill Mr. Samuel Brown? It doesn't right make any sense, knowing of his past atrocities and all."

"It's right in front of you, Watson," said Holmes, nodding at the engine.

"This? The infamous Ripper killed him for his invention? Why did he leave it then?"

"Not for the possession of it but to prevent it from seeing the light of day."

"What is it, Holmes?"

"If my deductions are correct, and I have no reason to believe they are not, it is a kerosene combustion engine."

"All right, Holmes." Dr. Watson crossed his arms. "What does a combustion engine have to do with Jack the Ripper?"

"Right now, our chief concern is a house keeper named Miss O'Brien, who may be in danger as we speak. If the people pulling the Ripper's strings become aware that she is alive . . ."

"Oh, heavens."

"We need to find her, Watson."

"And once we find her, Holmes? What then?"

"She's going to be the bait in our trap, of course."

CHAPTER FOUR: The Trap Is Set and Sprung

Thomas Quincy was a man comfortable in the dark, perhaps far too comfortable. When he returned to the home of Samuel Brown, he didn't bring a lantern or a phosphorus torch. Instead he moved along the shadowed confines of the streets that connected this dingy flat over the meat pie shop to the Brown home and once there watched. Standing across the street and in the mouth of an alley, he watched and waited, taking note of the single candle light that moved from window to window, then up stairs and back down again. The wind picked up and a bank of clouds rolled in to conceal the waxing moon. Thomas smelled the rain in the air, and it wouldn't be long before he would get wet.

Unless, of course, he was *inside*.

Only one candle moved about its business. After ensuring there was only one occupant, he crossed the street three blocks down and worked his way back up. Slipping to the rear corner of the adjoining house, and then slipped over the dividing wall, dropping to the ground within a stone's throw of the converted greenhouse workshop of the late Mr. Samuel Brown IV. With a glance left and right he pulled his working accoutrements from an inside coat pocket and within a dozen beats of his even-tempered heart, he deftly picked the door's locking mechanism, slid sideways through the doorframe and into pitch black. Recalling the layout of the workshop, he moved carefully, probing with his feet and fingertips until positioning himself into the corner nearest the door leading into the house proper. As he took his position, rain began falling and its rapping could be heard on the roof and age darkened windows. A far off roll of thunder pealed. Then, rotating his wrist, he released the blade he kept spring loaded in his sleeve into his hand and began to wait.

From watching her movements, Thomas was confident she turned down the house. With the late Mr. Brown no longer in residence, the house would be unused and if Irish whores were anything, they were stubborn wenches. He could imagine her saying it was the right and proper thing to do in their subhuman filthy way and, without being aware, his arm stabbed at his mind's apparition and stuck himself in the leg. He hissed through his teeth at the brief pain and loss of control. If she didn't appear quickly he may have to go looking for her. Not his preferred method. He liked to set and spring the trap. Wait until they wandered in too close.

As a boy, he had watched a feral cat, in a lot behind his father's estate, over the length of an afternoon. The cat had laid in wait for a red squirrel that was gathering black walnuts for the winter, motionless in a stand of grass, as the creature went about its work. Thomas didn't know if the cat had taken it into account or it was blind luck that placed a walnut within inches of that particular stand of grass, but when the red squirrel had finally worked its way to the nut in front of the grass, and picked up its prize, and turned away. A quick pounce, a bite across the back of the neck, and it was all over. The cat laid in wait for nearly three hours, but in the end, the cat's meal had come to *it*. The following day, Thomas returned to the lot with a saucer of milk and when the feral cat worked its way to where the saucer was positioned beneath the black walnut tree that had supplied the red squirrel, Thomas dropped the brick he carried up the tree with him, instantly crushing the cat's skull.

He noted from the pocket watch he stole from his father earlier that day that he himself had lain in wait for approximately an hour and a half before springing his own lethal trap.

And that pleased him immensely.

Lost for a moment in the memory, Thomas relaxed, breathing slow and deep. He would wait. She would come. Then echoing footfalls from the house and then a sliver of light escaped from beneath the door. Outside the storm was full upon them and a flash of lightning temporarily lit the room from the window. He was ready, excited. He would have to pay a call to a working girl after this was all said and done. The thrill he got from performing the hunt charged all his vices.

The door opened cautiously with candle and outstretched arm appearing first. She wore her uniform. Even with her employer dead and gone, the stupid stubborn Irish whore did what was proper. Thomas rolled the blade with the tips of his fingers.

That's a good girl. Step into the room. Better see what's in that far corner. Perfect.

Thomas moved quickly, silently. As he slipped in behind her, a great flash of light and boom shook the house, and if Miss O'Brien had been paying any attention she would have seen in the flash of lightning the form of Thomas Quincy, known to the papers years prior as the infamous Jack the Ripper, descend upon his prey. As he moved, part of his mind did note that she didn't startle at the thunder, expecting that in her current state she would have leapt straight from her shoes, but in the time it took for him to notice that small, but very important detail, he was against her back, having wrapped an arm around front and up tight against her neck.

"Good night my sweet smelling whore," he whispered into her ear. She went rigid and un- moving with fear, thrusting his blade into the high spot between the ribs that would give access to the rear cockles of her heart.

"Don't let the bed bugs—"

He stopped short in his farewell.

Reaching up, taking hold of his arm around her throat, she squeezed hard – inhumanly hard – pulling his arm off from around her – despite his leverage – all the while spinning underneath his arm, maintaining her firm hold of it, and soon bent his arm turned out and in front of him.

"What the hell?" Lightning and thunder boomed and flashed again to light the room, the candle hav- ing been dropped and snuffed out, and Thomas saw that she was not the Irish trollop that had taken hold of him, but a woman dressed up as her.

"Just like a man," she sneered, with a strong hint of rolling Teutonic accent. "Here, let me help you with that."

Thomas felt very much like the cat of his memories while she effortlessly snapped his arm with a deft turn of her wrist.

"Auughk!"

"No crying there," she commanded. "Not quite the same when a girl fights back, is it?"

"Elizabeth!"

Flashing lights revealed Holmes, Dr. Watson (with trusty revolver in hand, no less), and Miss O'Brien bursting into the room. Thomas saw that the woman he had stabbed looked nothing like his intended victim, unnaturally pale, yet seemingly larger than life than her average height would attest to. Her eyes dark and steely, her other vise-like hand still clutching him by the throat as he cradled his useless, broken arm, transfixed upon his knife still seeming to harmlessly protrude out of her back. She continued to squeeze.

"Enough," said Holmes. "He is beaten."

The woman identified as Elizabeth stopped squeezing, but still held Thomas firm in her inhuman grasp. "And what of those women that he so callously slaughtered for his own sick enjoyment, eh? Do you think they asked him to stop? While he cut them from stem to stern do you think their eyes did not beg for mercy as his are now?" She started squeezing again.

"Gllllkkkkkkkk!!!!" Thomas turned a rather unhealthy color, sweating profusely.

"Justice is not yours to decide in this matter," said Holmes, calmly. "He will be tried in a court of his peers. They will find him guilty and he will most surely hang."

Elizabeth's demeanor softened. "Too good for him. He should suffer." She gave a quick squeeze and Thomas collapsed, tossed to floor as if garbage.

"ELIZABETH!"

"He will live, Mr. Holmes, sadly, he will live." She turned, the protruding knife becoming visible to all.

"Good Lord, you've been stabbed!" shouted Dr. Watson, rushing forward. "Lie down. I'm a doctor." He turned. "Miss O'Brien, we'll need clean bandages!"

Miss O'Brien merely stood there gaping as Dr. Watson moved to take Elizabeth's arm.

"You would do well to remove your hands be-fore I assist you." Obviously, she was in no state of pain whatsoever.

It was now Dr. Watson's turn to gape at her, dumbfounded. "Why, I—"

"I have no need for your help." After waving him off, she turned away before realizing she could not reach the knife herself.

Silent and in awe, Dr. Watson noted the knife's position. A normal woman would have easily been slain outright by such a horrific wound. Yet here this woman still stood, vibrant and quite full of life.

Elizabeth sighed with a frown. "Ah. I see. Please. Do it." She turned her back to Dr. Watson, offering the plunged knife to him.

Dr. Watson grimaced while wrenching the knife out her back, still amazed that the supposed injury did not seem to affect her in the least. "Fascinating," was his only reply.

"Ahem," interjected Holmes, noting the awe and horror upon his friend's face. "Perhaps you could send for the Yard, Watson. I believe we have the matter in hand here."

"O-of course. If—if you'll excuse me, ladies." And with that, a stunned Dr. Watson left the room, clamoring out the door into the alley.

Holmes gently approached Miss O'Brien, still white as a sheet. "Miss O'Brien, may I introduce you to your temporary double, Elizabeth von Frankenstein."

Miss O'Brien blinked. "*The* Frankenstein?" she gasped, clearly taken aback.

"My cousin, and by marriage only," Elizabeth pointed out.

"The Frankenstein's were an acquaintance of Mary Shelly through Lord Byron before the events of the book many, many years ago," explained Holmes, hoping the facts would help ease the tension of the situation. "To prevent further scandal Mary Shelly wrote of the things that took place, but left out what became of Elizabeth after her supposed lethal encounter with her husband's famed creation, who, I dare say, is reported to still be active today. Victor used the knowledge he had gained and—"

"And he made me into another of his monsters," interrupted Elizabeth.

"But y-you . . . y-you're not . . ." stammered Miss O'Brien.

"I'm not, shall we say, hideous?" answered Elizabeth with a soft laugh. "Not to the naked eye, no."

"I want to thank you for your assistance, Elizabeth," interjected Holmes. "You have done a good thing here today. A very good thing."

She nearly sneered. "Good? Is that my true nature then? To be good? To do . . . good?"

"I believe it is what you wish it to be, yes." Holmes paused, scrutinizing Thomas's crumpled form.

"Excuse me, but, didn't you love him?" spoke up Miss O'Brien, now finding her courage. "You speak of him with such vitriol."

"Victor?"

"Yes, Victor, your husband."

"I loved him, yes. Even when he left on our wedding night to continue his precious work, I loved him. When his creature crept into our half-empty bridal room and told me I was to be his punishment, I loved him. When I awoke on his laboratory table? Well, you could say I then had a change of heart."

"Oh, God," gasped Miss O'Brien.

"No," corrected Elizabeth. "Not God. Just Victor."

"Elizabeth has taken residence in London and now assists me on occasion since my . . . return," said Holmes. "She has proven invaluable on many occasions and has taken upon herself to advocate for women in need of help."

Miss O'Brien clutched at her throat. "Is that true? Can it be possible that the ache I feel, the home I built in my heart for Samuel could be removed and replaced on the table of a doctor?"

Holmes shook his head. "I don't believe that's something you would want and I'm sure it is something that Mr. Brown would have frowned upon." He paused, reflecting upon the sentiment. "A fascinating question though, does love truly reside in the heart?"

The door to the city flew open, and there stood a frowning Watson.

"Remarkably quick, Watson," said Holmes stepping forward, immediately recognizing the look upon his friend's face. "Unless, of course, you never made it there. Ah, I see. Don't be rude, Mycroft, come in and I will introduce you."

Entering the room now was an older, much larger and stouter man who greatly resembled the great detective, yet above his unwieldy frame perched a head so masterful in its brow, so alert in its steel-gray, deep-set eyes, so firm in its lips, and so subtle in its play of expression, that after the first glance one forgot the gross body and remembered only the dominant mind in control.

"Impressive as always, Sherlock," said the heavily built and massive man, smiling.

Holmes let out a half-sigh. "Miss O'Brien, Elizabeth, allow me to introduce Mycroft Holmes, head of Her Majesty's Secret Service, amongst other things. It is my privilege to be his younger brother of seven years, but like most siblings we occasionally have a difference of opinion, like what he is about tell me I must do."

Mycroft smiled. "Baroness Elizabeth Von Frankenstein. It appears the account of your demise was greatly exaggerated."

"No. It wasn't," she replied.

Mycroft chuckled. "Absolutely fascinating. It is indeed a pleasure and an honor to meet you Baroness."

"Any claim I had to that title died with me," said Elizabeth, now glowering.

Mycroft gave a slight nod of his impressive balding head. "Of course, of course. I only defer to it, because of the grace and presence you carry yourself with. You are a baroness in all but title."

"Very kind of you," said Elizabeth. "Shall I refer to you as the Donkey Mycroft Holmes then?"

"Mycroft, Elizabeth, please," soothed Holmes.

"Grace, beauty, and a barbed tongue." Again Mycroft gave a low chuckle. "I'm sure you are the 'life' of every party. I don't imagine you'd be interested in sharing what you know of Victor's work with some of my colleagues, now, would you?"

"Not in the least."

"Pity. Ah, well." Mycroft clutched his lapels. "We will piece it together in the end. Your help would have only sped along our efforts."

"Then I find myself in your debt," said Elizabeth.

"However so?" asked Mycroft, dropping his hands.

"Before this instant, I wondered how I would be spending my evenings. I've now booked them with making sure you never recreate Victor's work."

Mycroft gave a wolfish smile. "Then I look forward to crossing swords with you—rhetorical or otherwise, your choice." He then softened, turning his attention elsewhere. "Miss O'Brien, my condolences on your loss. Mr. Brown was a jewel in England's crown of brilliant minds."

"H-how do you know matters between Samuel and myself, sir?" asked Miss O'Brien.

Holmes clicked his tongue. "My brother is the keeper of a hundred secrets and as the American Ben Franklin said, 'A secret is kept between three, only if two are dead.' I'm afraid you will only get misdirection and innuendo from my brother, Miss O'Brien— like the obsufication of his true purpose here and the interception of Dr. Watson's mission."

"No such thing, Sherlock," said Mycroft, dismissing Holmes with causal gesture. "To answer your question, Miss O'Brien, I will allow my dear younger brother the honors, since I suspect he has pieced it all together himself. Sherlock? The stage is yours, as they say."

"Mycroft, or rather, he and his predecessors have been watching Mr. Brown's family for generations now."

"How so?" asked Miss O'Brien.

"Samuels's namesake, his great grandfather Samuel Brown, originally invented this remarkable engine as early as 1824 . . ."

"1825," corrected Mycroft.

"And our government, in its esteemed . . . wisdom, later purchased the rights to the invention with the intention that Mr. Brown never reveal its existence to the general public, with hopes to protect the capital and social interests associated with the further development of steam technology. Earlier, when Watson and I discovered his scientific journal, I noticed that the handwriting was different in the later entries than in the earlier and that the dates therein went back to the 1820s, abruptly stopping in late 1824, and then resuming in 1889, four years ago."

"Yes," said Mycroft, "Mr. Brown applied for a patent only a few short months ago and—"

"Which was discovered by parties hostile to Mr. Brown's inherited ingenuity, and set in motion a plan to stop him from succeeding," continued Holmes.

"And when news of his murder reached my ears," added Mycroft, "I assisted in the case behind the scenes, knowing full well Sherlock would become involved and flush out the murderer in his own interminable style."

"Which brings us to your being here in person now," said Holmes.

"Correct," answered Mycroft.

Elizabeth balled her hands into fists. "You can't have him."

"She is quick, Sherlock," noted Mycroft. "I understand your affinity."

"What is he talking about, Holmes?" asked a bewildered Dr. Watson. "Why would Mycroft, of all people, be here to collect this killer?"

"Thomas Quincy is in the direct employ of the ministry," answered Mycroft, matter-of-factly.

"Thomas Quincy is Jack the Ripper!" protested Elizabeth, now livid with rage. "One of the most heinous murderers in history, English or other-wise?!"

Mycroft held up his hand. "He could very well be Vlad the Impaler or Guy Fawkes, but he *is* protected. You turn him over to the Yard and there are people *not* of my branch who will insure he is out and gone before they serve him his first meal. He will be gone and the people protecting him will disappear as well. There is a growing cancer in the Queen's government and it is an elusive and virulent strain. Without a known high ranking member in play we may never find how much of England's body is infected."

"His breathing has changed," interjected Holmes. "He's waking up."

Thomas stirred. "Uhhhnnn . . ."

Elizabeth stepped forward, ready to crush his neck with her feet, if need be: "I will kill him myself."

"No," said Holmes.

"No?" returned Elizabeth. "And how would you stop me, Sherlock?"

Thomas warily got back onto his feet, still clutching his throat, panting.

"Sherlock understands sometimes England needs to be protected, sometimes even from herself," stated Mycroft. "Thomas Quincy is an invaluable resource that will be, must be protected. It is not a perfect outcome, but it is the outcome you and he must accept."

"No." Holmes raised his clockwork arm, point-ing his palm at Thomas. Four shots rang out.

Thomas twirled about, and collapsed once again.

Miss O'Brien screamed, fainting away, luckily caught by the nearby Dr. Watson, safely pulling her off to the side.

"Sherlock!" shouted Mycroft.

"Holmes!" cried Dr. Watson, gently setting down his charge.

"What have you done?" asked Mycroft in amazement. "What has become of you?"

"I am serving the justice you would see him elude," said Holmes, icily.

Thomas stirred once again.

"Thank goodness," breathed Mycroft.

Thomas stood as four smashed bullets fell from his chest.

"Body armor," half-whispered Holmes.

"I never leave without it," laughed Thomas in a raspy voice, obviously bruised, and nursing cracked ribs.

Holmes bent his wrist and four shells ejected from his sleeve. He reached for his pocket to reload.

Mycroft clicked his tongue. "I'm sorry, Sher-lock, but I cannot allow you to transgress against him any further." He drew a small pistol from his vest, aiming it squarely at Holmes's head. "You know very well that I am an expert marksman."

Dr. Watson drew out his revolver. "And you, sir, are a much larger and easier to hit target."

Mycroft chortled. "Touché, my good Dr. Wat-son. Touché." He resumed his serious tone and demeanor. "Nonetheless." He cocked the pistol.

"Hurrrrr!" Elizabeth advanced towards Mycroft, but the more agile Holmes shifted himself between the two, holding her back.

"Don't," he said.

"I'm sorry it has come to this, Sherlock. I thought you a rock of reason. I see that your un-fortunate condition has unhinged your faculties." He turned to Thomas. "Can you walk?"

"Oh, yes," replied Thomas with a moan. "Gladly."

"Then leave," ordered Mycroft. "Don't stop until you are sure you are in safe company."

Thomas nodded, and then a cruel grin stretched itself upon his twisted face. "Well, it has been a delight." He swayed at Dr. Watson. "Give my best to the lady. Tell her I'm sorry things didn't work out between us." He then blew Elizabeth a kiss. "I owe you. I'd sleep with the light on if I was you."

Elizabeth lunged forward, snarling, only to be held back once again by Holmes. "You are sorely mistaken if you think you'd be the scariest thing I have ever had in my bed chamber," growled Elizabeth.

"Just not your evening is it, Holmes?" sniggered Thomas, turning to the detective. "Slipped through your fingers once again, haven't I?" Holmes stood motionless, steely eyed as Thomas gloated further. "Maybe next time, eh? Ha! With that, I will bid you all adieu." He then limped through the open door way, disappearing into the night.

There was a long, tense, silent moment.

Holmes broke the silence, directing his comment at Mycroft. "'Unhinged my faculties?' Really?"

"A tad too much?" offered Mycroft. "I was attempting a rather realism, you know."

"It's good to know you're confident in the bonds of brotherhood," said Holmes.

"And I yours," countered Mycroft. "And I yours."

"Holmes? What on earth?" asked Dr. Watson, scratching his head.

"Apologies, my good Watson, my brother and I were practicing the art of the dramatic."

"We are quite good at it, you know," added Mycroft.

"Quite," agreed Holmes.

Miss O'Brien stirred.

Dr. Watson helped her up. "Easy, miss."

"Would you two care to explain yourselves?" said Elizabeth, tersely, clearly still agitated.

"I believe my brother has one more act up his ample sleeve to perform, don't you, Mycroft?"

"Of course," said Mycroft. "I warned that insufferable, little, thin prat to be mindful, didn't I?" He paused. "Dr. Griffin?

A phantom voice replied. "Yes?"

"Follow him," ordered Mycroft as the others, save Holmes, looked on in astonishment. "Note anyone and everyone he speaks with and where."

"I will report back to you directly," replied the phantom voice.

"And, Dr. Griffin . . ." continued Mycroft.

"Yes, sir?"

"Once he goes to ground or they move to send him out of the country—"

"Yes?"

"It would be a shame if he had a poorly timed twist of the ankle," suggested Mycroft, his eyes narrowing. "People have been killed under the wheels of a carriage with the bad luck of a poorly placed step or jostle. Even in the middle of a busy street with a dozen people unable to stop it and to comment on the random accidental nature of it."

"I understand," said Dr. Griffin. "Completely."

"Good. I knew you would. Now, off with you."

And the door suddenly flung open and as quickly shut itself as the Invisible Man went about his task at hand.

"Incredible. Impossible," breathed Dr. Watson, holstering his revolver with a trembling hand.

"All things being equal, I would only give it a remarkable," noted Holmes.

"I thought it was merely novel at best," nonchalantly added Mycroft, giving a slight shrug.

Miss O'Brien was nearly on the edge of hyper-ventilating, swaying to and fro. "I-I don't under-stand all this. Any of it. What happened? Where's the man Mr. Holmes shot? Why did the door open and close by itself? What happened? Where's the man who killed my Samuel?"

"My apologies, Miss O'Brien," offered Holmes. "My brother and I get involved when we're in each other's presence. It was rude. Allow me to explain. My brother Mycroft works for her majesty's government although you would be hard pressed to find an office door with his name on it. He's a problem solver for problems that have yet to occur, if you can understand that. I knew it was a poss-ibility he would become involved when I put information into the ether to bait our trap. The bait attracted not only our prey, but larger predators as well. When Mycroft arrived, I thought he was holding the door behind Watson for his inflated sense of the dramatic—"

"Hmp. Calling the kettle black," interrupted Mycroft.

"When in fact there were three in their impromptu party," continued Holmes. "I wouldn't have noticed anything else except when I believed the Elizabeth had squeezed the life from our dubious Mr. Quincy because I couldn't see the rise and fall of his chest. When she told me he was still alive, I focused on my other senses, not visually confirming his breathing, but listening for it. That's when I discovered a seventh person in the room, standing behind Mycroft and a heavy smoker of clove cigarettes. There was a slight wheeze to his breathing that made it very distinct and noticeable. Then as my brother pleaded his case for taking Mr. Quincy into his custody, he asked that we allow him to be used as the cheese for an even bigger trap."

"I'm afraid I missed that part," admitted Dr. Watson, still a bit shaken by the recent events. "When *exactly* did he request that?"

"Well, not in so many words, Watson," said Holmes. "He was moving in that direction in his roundabout fashion—"

"Can't imagine," sighed Elizabeth.

"Touché," countered Holmes. "He was about to ask when our killer began to awake and the game was afoot."

"But you tried to kill him," said Dr. Watson,

"Ah, but I didn't. I realized that because I couldn't see his chest rise and fall there was something with a rigid form beneath his clothing."

"Armor," said Dr. Watson, wistfully.

"Correct and since I knew that Mr. Quincy was a knife man, he would be acutely aware of the disadvantages of bringing a knife to a gun fight, indicating armor designed to stop bullets."

"You still haven't explained why you shot him," demanded Elizabeth.

"Mr. Quincy is an intelligent adversary, as shown by his elusiveness during our first en-counters," continued Holmes. "He was aware of the formidable powers that worked against him and if he was allowed to just walk out, I'm positive he would have known it was a trap and gone into hiding. By my staged attempt to kill him—"

"Speaking of which, how does one eject casings from their undercoat?" asked Mycroft, pointing. "I am more than quite curious about the applications and working of whatever it is you have under there."

"A twenty-two pepperbox installed in the fore-arm courtesy of one Dr. Jekyll—"

"Ah. Well, good thing we already have him under retainer, then, seeing as we still have to keep a keen eye on him as well, it seems."

"Please continue, how did you . . . ?" asked Elizabeth, shifting about, growing more impatient.

"My apologies, Elizabeth," said Holmes. "If Mr. Quincy believed he had narrowly escaped death by his own contingency and then witnessed brothers turn against one another under the auspice of a powerful patronage, apparently providing him with *carte blanche*, he would believe himself untouch-able."

"And instead of hiding, he would strut and preen his way back to the people holding his strings," said Elizabeth. "Ah, I see."

"Keen and beautiful." Mycroft leaned in on his toes. "More enchanting by the moment."

"Flattery won't weaken my resolve, Mycroft," said Elizabeth with a polite sneer. "I will stop your plans of continuing Victor's work."

"And determined as well. Ah, I do so look forward to our future encounters my dear, be sure of that. Now if you will excuse me, I have a government to save and all that." Mycroft gave a small bow. "Sherlock. Dr. Watson. Miss O'Brien. Baroness." And then he too went out the door and into the night.

"I believe Miss O'Brien could do with a spot of gin to put a bit of color back into her cheeks," said Holmes. "Watson, could you be kind enough to see to her this evening and assist her with her travel plans on the morrow?"

"Of course, Holmes," replied Dr. Watson. "Of course."

"Where are you going?" Elizabeth asked Miss O'Brien, truly interested in her plight.

"Mr. Holmes has arranged for safe passage to America," she answered, still visibly a bit stunned.

Elizabeth shook her head. "She has survived this ordeal only to be banished to another country. How typical."

"Not in the least," said Dr. Watson with a smile. "Miss O'Brien is now the sole owner of the Samuel Brown family legacy kerosene combustion engine, which waits for her on a steamer departing tomorrow morning. There is a pair of American entrepreneurs who are very interested in the design and are willing to bring Miss O'Brien in as a partner in mass producing them. Although Mr. Brown's invention found no desired welcome in England, I believe it will have a home in the new world. And seeing as Mycroft did not mention it at all in that sense, we can only imagine her departure with the device carries his blessing as well."

"Or as my Da would tell ya, 'Tis easier to ask forgiveness than it is permission,'" concluded Miss O'Brien.

"Couldn't have expressed it better myself," said Holmes. "Now if you'll excuse me, my presence has been requested for a late supper and a moonlit stroll along the Thames."

"Oh, splendid. And yourself, Elizabeth?" asked Dr. Watson.

"I did the requesting," said she.

"Good heavens!" exclaimed Dr. Watson. "You – you're a two!"

"Pardon me?" asked Elizabeth.

Holmes gallantly took Elizabeth by the arm. "It is a brave new world, Dr. Watson, both dark and wondrous, and I wouldn't miss it for the world. Good evening, Watson."

Dr. Watson smiled. "Good evening, Holmes."

THE END

AUTHOR BIOS

Roy C. Booth is a published author, comedian, poet, journalist, essayist, screenwriter, and internationally awarded playwright with nearly 60 plays published (Samuel French, Heuer, *et al*) with nearly 800 productions worldwide in 28 countries in ten languages. Also known for collaborations with R Thomas Riley, Brian Keene, Eric M. Heideman, William F. Wu, and others (along with his presence on the regional convention circuit), Roy hails from Bemidji, MN where he also manages Roy's Comics & Games with his wife, Cynthia, and his three sons, Riordan, Rex, and Revelin. More of Roy's work can be found on Amazon at:

www.amazon.com/author/roycbooth

Nicholas Johnson lives in Mankato, MN with his wife Erica and his two children, Zoe and Sam.

66480016R00064

Made in the USA
Columbia, SC
17 July 2019